MW00762527

Hear the Angels Sing

featuring the artwork of

Lynn Bywaters, Judith Ann Griffith,
and Jennifer St. Denis

Ideals Children's Books • Nashville, Tennessee

Published by Ideals Publishing Corporation
Nashville, Tennessee 37214

Printed and bound in the United States of America.

ISBN 0-8249-7630-4 (book/cassette pkg.)
ISBN 0-8249-8624-5 (book only)

The display type is set in Phyllis and Phyllis Initials.
The text type is set in Galliard.
Color separations were made by Rayson Films, Inc., Waukesha, Wisconsin.
Printed and bound by Worzalla Publishing, Stevens Point, Wisconsin.

Designed by Stacy Venturi-Pickett.

First Edition
10 9 8 7 6 5 4 3 2 1

Table of Contents

Hark! the Herald Angels Sing 5
O Come, All Ye Faithful...7
The First Noel 8
While Shepherds Watched Their Flocks by Night 11
Angels We Have Heard on High.....................................13
O Holy Night..17
Angels, from the Realms of Glory 18
God Rest You Merry, Gentlemen 21
Silent Night...23
Shepherds! Shake off Your Drowsy Sleep........................27
O Little Town of Bethlehem 29
It Came upon the Midnight Clear..................................31

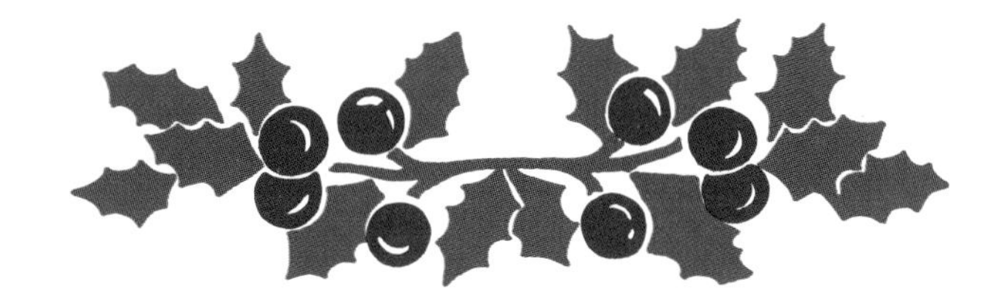

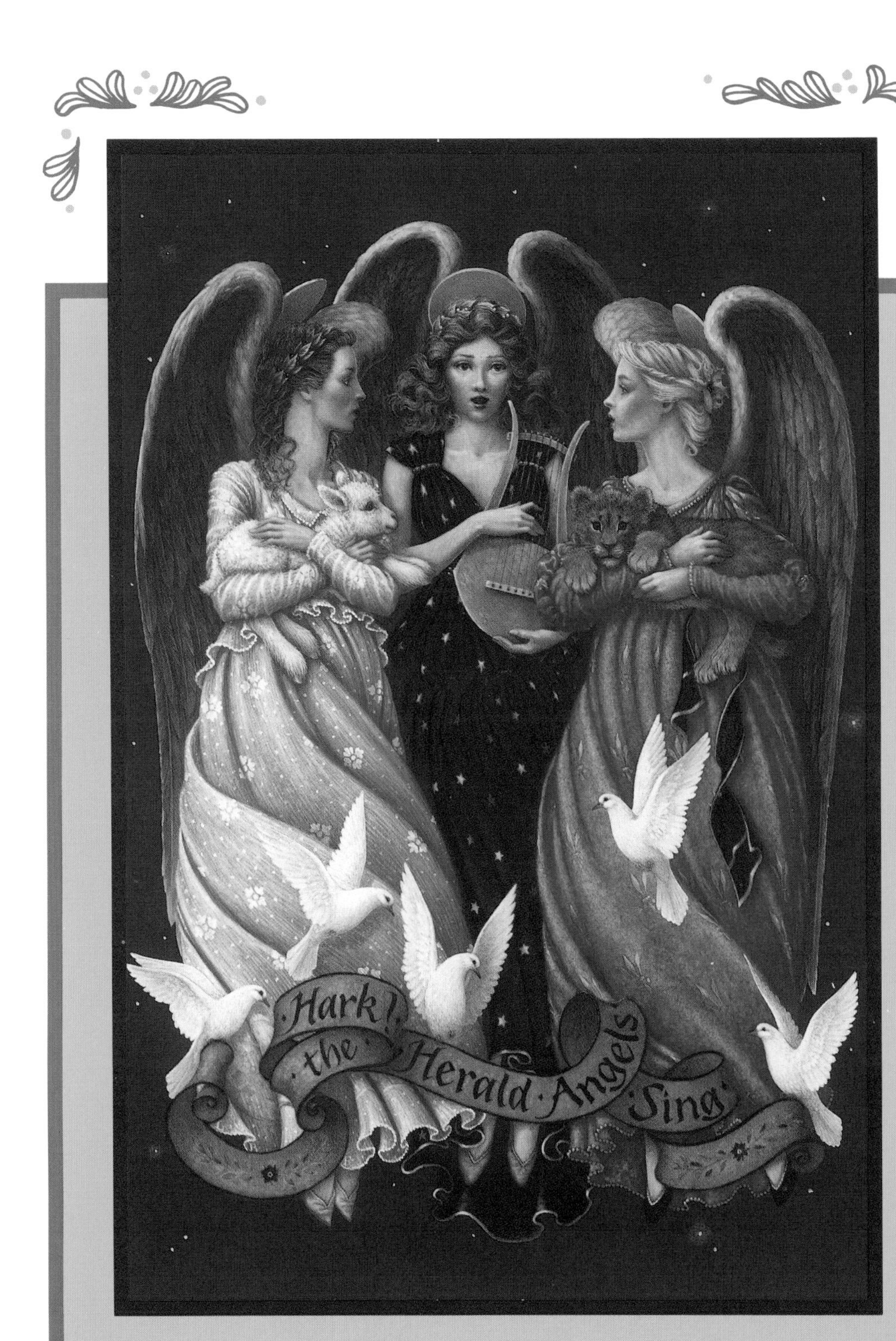
Hark! the Herald Angels Sing

Hark! the Herald Angels Sing

Charles Wesley

Hark! the herald angels sing,
"Glory to the newborn King:
Peace on earth and mercy mild,
God and sinners reconciled!"
Joyful all ye nations, rise,
Join the triumph of the skies;
With th'angelic host proclaim,
"Christ is born in Bethlehem!"
Hark! The herald angels sing,
"Glory to the newborn King."

Christ, by highest heav'n adored;
Christ, the everlasting Lord!
Late in time behold Him come,
Offspring of the favored one;
Veiled in flesh the Godhead see,
Hail th'incarnate deity,
Pleased as man with men to dwell,
Jesus our Emmanuel.
Hark! The herald angels sing,
"Glory to the newborn King."

Hail the heav'n-born Prince of Peace!
Hail the Son of Righteousness!
Light and life to all He brings,
Ris'n with healing in His wings.
Mild He lays His glory by.
Born that man no more may die,
Born to raise the sons of earth,
Born to give them second birth.
Hark! The herald angels sing,
"Glory to the newborn King."

Joyful all ye nations, rise,
Join the triumph of the skies;
With th'angelic host proclaim,
"Christ is born in Bethlehem!"
Hark! The herald angels sing,
"Glory to the newborn King."

O Come, All Ye Faithful

Tr. by F. Oakeley, 1852

O come, all ye faithful, joyful and triumphant,
O come ye, o come ye to Bethlehem;
Come and behold Him, born the king of angels:
O come, let us adore Him,
O come, let us adore Him,
O come, let us adore Him, Christ the Lord.

Sing, choirs of angels, sing in exultation,
Sing, all ye citizens of heaven above;
Glory to God, all glory in the highest:
O come, let us adore Him,
O come, let us adore Him,
O come, let us adore Him, Christ the Lord.

Yea, Lord, we greet Thee, born this happy morning,
Jesus to Thee be all glory giv'n;
Word of the Father now in flesh appearing:
O come, let us adore Him,
O come, let us adore Him,
O come, let us adore Him, Christ the Lord.

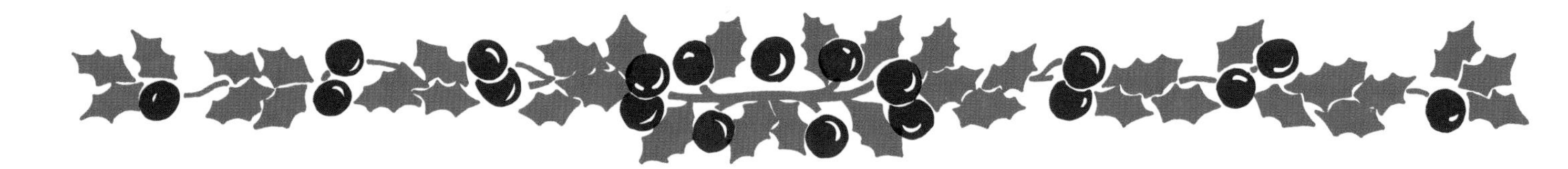

The First Noel

Traditional

The first noel, the angel did say,
Was to certain poor shepherds in fields as they lay;
In fields where they lay keeping their sheep,
On a cold winter's night that was so deep.
Noel, Noel, Noel, Noel!
Born is the King of Israel!

They looked up and saw a star
Shining in the east beyond them far.
And to the earth it gave great light,
And so it continued both day and night.
Noel, Noel, Noel, Noel!
Born is the King of Israel!

And by the light of that same star,
Three wise men came from country far;
To seek for a King was their intent,
And to follow the star wherever it went.
Noel, Noel, Noel, Noel!
Born is the King of Israel!

While Shepherds Watched Their Flocks by Night

Rev. Nahum Tate

While shepherds watched their flocks by night,
All seated on the ground,
The angel of the Lord came down,
And glory shone around,
And glory shone around.

"Fear not!" said he; for mighty dread
Had seized their troubled mind.
"Glad tidings of great joy I bring,
To you and all mankind,
To you and all mankind."

"The Heav'nly Babe you there shall find
To human view displayed,
All meanly wrapped in swathing bands,
And in a manger laid,
And in a manger laid."

"All glory be to God on high,
And to the earth be peace:
Goodwill hence forth from heav'n to men,
Begin and never cease,
Begin and never cease."

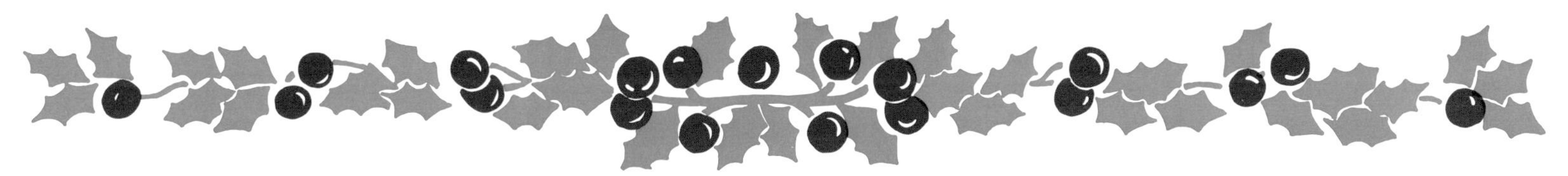

Angels We Have Heard on High

Traditional

Angels we have heard on high,
Sweetly singing o'er the plains;
And the mountains in reply
Echoing their joyous strains.
Gloria in excelsis Deo,
Gloria in excelsis Deo.

Shepherds, why this jubilee?
Why your joyous songs prolong?
What the gladsome tidings be
Which inspire your heav'nly song?
Gloria in excelsis Deo,
Gloria in excelsis Deo.

Gloria in excelsis Deo,
Gloria in excelsis Deo.

·JUDITH·

O Holy Night

J.S. Dwight

O holy night! The stars are brightly shining,
It is the night of the dear Savior's birth;
Long lay the world in sin and sorrow pining,
Till He appeared, and the soul felt its worth.
A thrill of hope, the weary world rejoices,
For yonder breaks a new and glorious morn!
Fall on your knees!
O hear the angel voices!
O night divine!
O night when Christ was born!
O night divine! O night, o night divine!

Truly He taught us to love one another;
His law is love and His gospel is peace;
Chains shall He break, for the slave is our brother,
And in His name, all oppression shall cease.
With hymns of joy in grateful chorus raising,
Let every heart adore His Holy Name!
Christ is the Lord!
With saint and seraph praising,
His power and glory evermore proclaim!
His power and glory evermore proclaim!

Fall on your knees!
O hear the angel voices!
O night divine!
O night when Christ was born!
O night divine! O night, o night divine!

Angels, from the Realms of Glory

James Montgomery

Angels, from the realms of glory,
Wing your flight o'er all the earth;
Ye who sang creation's story,
Now proclaim Messiah's birth:
Come and worship,
Come and worship,
Worship Christ, the newborn King.

Come and worship,
Come and worship,
Worship Christ, the newborn King.

Shepherds, in the fields abiding,
Watching o'er your flocks by night,
God with man is now residing;
Yonder shines the infant Light:
Come and worship,
Come and worship,
Worship Christ, the newborn King.

Sages, leave your contemplations,
Brighter visions beam afar;
Seek the great desire of nations;
Ye have seen His natal star:
Come and worship,
Come and worship,
Worship Christ, the newborn King.

Saints, before the altar bending,
Watching long in hope and fear,
Suddenly the Lord, descending,
In His temple shall appear:
Come and worship,
Come and worship,
Worship Christ, the newborn King.

Come and worship,
Come and worship,
Worship Christ, the newborn King.

God Rest You Merry, Gentlemen

Traditional

God rest you merry, gentlemen,
Let nothing you dismay.
Remember Christ our Savior
Was born on Christmas Day,
To save us all from Satan's power
When we were gone astray.
O tidings of comfort and joy,
Comfort and joy,
O tidings of comfort and joy.

From God our Heav'nly Father
A blessed angel came,
And unto certain shepherds
Brought tidings of the same,
How that in Bethlehem was born
The Son of God by name.
O tidings of comfort and joy,
Comfort and joy,
O tidings of comfort and joy.

Now to the Lord sing praises,
All you within this place,
And with true love and brotherhood
Each other now embrace;
This holy tide of Christmas
All other doth deface.
O tidings of comfort and joy,
Comfort and joy,
O tidings of comfort and joy.

Silent Night

Joseph Möhr

Silent night! Holy Night!
All is calm, all is bright,
Round yon Virgin Mother and Child.
Holy Infant, so tender and mild.
Sleep in heavenly peace,
Sleep in heavenly peace.

Silent night! Holy night!
Shepherds quake at the sight;
Glories stream from heaven afar,
Heavenly hosts sing Alleluia,
Christ the Savior is born!
Christ the Savior is born!

Silent night! Holy night!
Son of God, love's pure light
Radiant beams from Thy holy face,
With the dawn of redeeming grace,
Jesus, Lord at Thy birth,
Jesus, Lord at Thy birth.

JUDITH

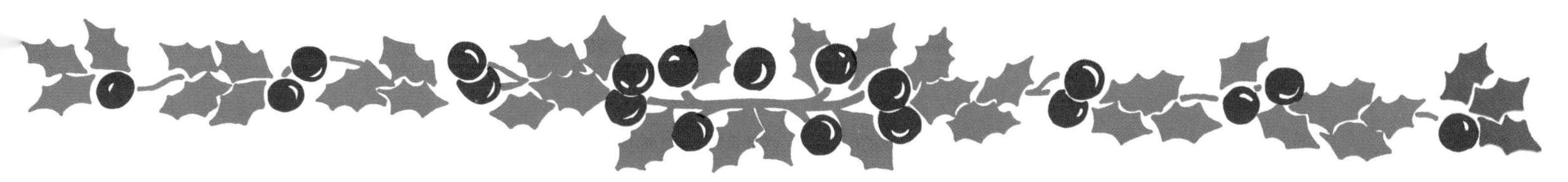

Shepherds! Shake off Your Drowsy Sleep

Traditional

Shepherds! Shake off your drowsy sleep,
Rise and leave your slumb'ring sheep.
Angels from Heav'n around loud singing,
Tidings of great joy are bringing,
Shepherds! The chorus come and swell!
Sing Noel, o sing Noel.

Cometh at length the age of peace,
Strife and sorrow now shall cease.
Prophets foretold the wondrous story
Of this Heaven born Prince of Glory
Shepherds! The chorus come and swell!
Sing Noel, o sing Noel.

Shepherds! Arise and quick away,
Seek the Babe at break of day.
He is the hope of every nation,
All in Him shall find salvation.
Shepherds! The chorus come and swell!
Sing Noel, o sing Noel.

O Little Town of Bethlehem

Rev. Phillips Brooks

O little town of Bethlehem,
How still we see thee lie!
Above thy deep and dreamless sleep
The silent stars go by;
Yet in thy dark streets shineth
The everlasting light;
The hopes and fears of all the years
Are met in thee tonight.

For Christ is born of Mary;
And gathered all above,
While mortals sleep the angels keep
Their watch of wond'ring love.
O morning stars together
Proclaim the holy birth,
And praises sing to God our King,
And peace to men on earth.

How silently, how silently
The wondrous gift is giv'n!
So God imparts to human hearts
The blessings of His heav'n.
No ear may hear His coming;
But in this world of sin,
Where meek souls will receive Him still,
The dear Christ enters in.

O Holy Child of Bethlehem
Descend to us, we pray;
Cast out our sin and enter in,
Be born in us today.
We hear the Christmas angels,
The great glad tidings tell;
O, come to us, abide with us,
Our Lord Emmanuel,
Our Lord Emmanuel.

It came upon a midnight clear
JUDITH

It Came upon the Midnight Clear

Edmund H. Sears

It came upon the midnight clear,
That glorious song of old,
From angels bending near the earth
To touch their harps of gold.
"Peace on the earth, good will to men,
From Heaven's all gracious King."
The world in solemn stillness lay
To hear the angels sing.

Still through the cloven skies they come
With peaceful wings unfurled.
And still their heav'nly music floats
O'er all the weary world;
Above its sad and lowly plains
They bend on hovering wing.
And ever o'er its Babel sounds
The blessed angels sing.

For lo, the days are hast'ning on,
By prophet seen of old,
When with the ever-circling years
Shall come the time foretold;
When the new heav'n and earth shall own
The Prince of Peace their King,
And the whole world send back the song
Which now the angels sing.

Index of First Lines

Angels, from the realms of glory, 18
Angels we have heard on high, 13
The first noel, the angel did say, 8
God rest you merry, gentlemen, 21
Hark! the herald angels sing, 5
It came upon the midnight clear, 31
O come, all ye faithful, joyful and triumphant, 7
O holy night! The stars are brightly shining, 17
O little town of Bethlehem, 29
Shepherds! Shake off your drowsy sleep, 27
Silent night! Holy night!, 23
While shepherds watched their flocks by night, 11

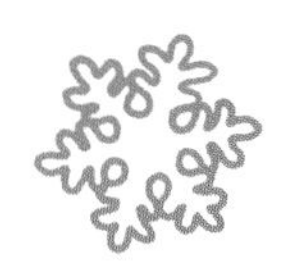